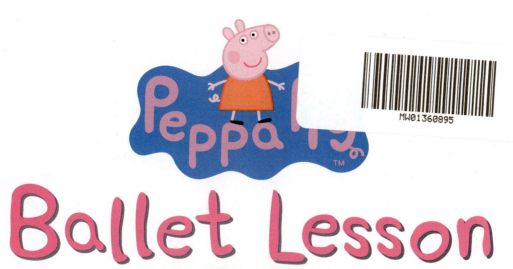

Ballet Lesson

SCHOLASTIC INC.

Adapted by Elizabeth Schaefer

No part of this publication may be reproduced, stored in a retrieval system, or transmitted in any form or by any means, electronic, mechanical, photocopying, recording, or otherwise, without written permission of the publisher. For information regarding permission, write to Scholastic Inc., Attention: Permissions Department, 557 Broadway, New York, NY 10012.

ISBN 978-0-545-74775-2

Published by arrangement with Entertainment One and Ladybird Books, A Penguin Company.
This book is based on the TV series *Peppa Pig*.
Peppa Pig is created by Neville Astley and Mark Baker.
Peppa Pig © Astley Baker Davies Ltd/Entertainment One UK Ltd 2003.

All rights reserved. Published by Scholastic Inc. SCHOLASTIC and associated logos are trademarks and/or registered trademarks of Scholastic Inc.

10 9 8 7 6 5 4 3 2   14 15 16 17 18 19/0

Printed in the U.S.A.   40
First Scholastic printing, August 2014

www.peppapig.com

Mummy Pig is taking Peppa to her first ballet lesson. Madame Gazelle greets them at the door. "You must be young Peppa," she says with a graceful bow.

"Hello, Madame," says Peppa.
Mummy Pig kisses Peppa good-bye. "I'll pick you up later. Enjoy yourself!"

Peppa's friends Candy Cat, Suzy Sheep, Danny Dog, Rebecca Rabbit, and Pedro Pony are already inside.

Madame Gazelle claps her hands. "Today we have a new pupil, Peppa Pig!"

It is time for the ballet lesson to begin. "We will start with a little jump," says Madame Gazelle. "A *petit jeté*."

Peppa watches as Madame Gazelle shows everyone how to jump like a ballerina.
"Leap with grace and beauty," Madame Gazelle tells the dancers.

Peppa and her friends try the little jump.
Thump! Thump!

Their feet make loud noises as they hit the floor! "Let's try it again," says Madame Gazelle. "Petit jeté. Grace and beauty!"

THUMP!

THUMP!

THUMP!

THUMP! THUMP! THUMP!

Peppa and her friends jump some more.

THUMP! THUMP!
The students are not as graceful as Madame Gazelle.
But everyone is having fun!

Madame Gazelle turns on some music and claps her hands. "Children, now let's pretend to dance like we are beautiful swans."

"What noise do you think a swan might make?" asks Madame Gazelle.

Peppa and her friends don't know what noise a swan makes. So they all make their own noises!

The dance lesson is finished. Mummy Pig comes to take Peppa home.

"Peppa did very well," Madame Gazelle says.
"Thank you, Madame." Peppa is very happy.

Hee!

Hee! Hee!

At home, Peppa wants to show her family what she has learned.

"I am going to teach you how to do ballet," Peppa announces.

"Is it difficult?" asks Daddy Pig.

"You must copy exactly what I do," says Peppa. "Madame Gazelle used funny words. But it's just bending your knees and jumping, really."

Peppa turns on some music and shows Mummy, Daddy, and George how to do a little jump. Daddy Pig smiles. "Ah, the *petit jeté*."

Snort!

"Daddy! You know the funny words!"
Ho Ho Ho!
"Mummy Pig and I used to be very good at ballet," says Daddy.

Daddy Pig and Mummy Pig dance together.
He lifts her up, just like a ballerina.

"Our favorite dance was the *pas de deux*," Daddy says. He tosses Mummy Pig high into the air. "That's a dance for two people."

THUMP! Oh, dear! Daddy doesn't catch Mummy in time. She lands on top of him!

"That wasn't quite how I remembered it," says Daddy.
Hee, Hee, Hee! Silly Daddy Pig!

"Maybe we should leave the ballet to Peppa," Daddy Pig says.

"Yes," says Peppa. "I am the best at it. I am like a beautiful swan!"

Peppa loves dancing. Everyone loves dancing!

Clap! Clap! Clap!